CW0093*150

Woodland Magic

OPERATION **OWL**

THE WOODLAND MAGIC SERIES

Woodland Magic

OPERATION OWL

JULIE SYKES
illustrated by KATY RIDDELL

Piccadilly
PRESS

First published in Great Britain in 2023 by
PICCADILLY PRESS
4th Floor, Victoria House, Bloomsbury Square, London WC1B 4DA
Owned by Bonnier Books
Sveavägen 56, Stockholm, Sweden
bonnierbooks.co.uk/PiccadillyPress

Text copyright © Julie Sykes, 2023
Illustrations copyright © Katy Riddell, 2023

This is a work of fiction. Names, places, events and incidents are either the
products of the author's imagination or used fictitiously. Any resemblance
to actual persons, living or dead, is purely coincidental.

A CIP catalogue record for this book is available from the British Library.

ISBN: 978-1-80078-145-0
Also available as an ebook and in audio

1

Typeset by Envy Design Ltd
Printed and bound in Great Britain by Clays Ltd, Elcograf S.p.A.

Piccadilly Press is an imprint of Bonnier Books UK
bonnierbooks.co.uk

Chapter One

'That's it. Time to go.' Cora emptied the leaves from her net into her woodland bag.

'But we've only cleared the floating leaves,' said Jax. 'There are still loads around the pond's edge.'

'Clearing the pond and the ground around it is a big task. Scarlet said we could have longer if we needed it.' Cora glanced at the sky as she added the net to her bag. The dark was melting away. Soon the sun would be up and with it the

Ruffins, stomping around on their huge
pongy feet. She shivered, remembering how
only a few weeks ago a Ruffin child had
caught and trapped her. Luckily for Cora,
her friends had found her and helped her
to escape, but it wasn't an experience she
wanted to repeat.

Cora fixed Jax with a look. 'If we don't
leave now, we might not make it back to the
Bramble Door before sunrise. We'll be locked
out of the Hidden Middle in daylight!'

Cora and Jax had been working on
Downy Common, the furthest they'd ever
been from the Whispering Woods. Scarlet
had sent them there because she'd finally
promoted Cora and Jax from trainees to
fully trained Keepers.

Jax gave in. He put his net and rake in
his woodland bag then slung it on his back.
'Race you home. Hi, lo, GO!'

They ran across the common and sprinted through a corn field. The corn had been harvested and the field ploughed. Cora and Jax jumped over the furrows as they ran towards a derelict barn at the field's edge. As they approached, a shape appeared in the barn doorway.

'Ruffin!' Cora dived, flattening herself in the middle of a furrow and hoping that the earthy ridges would be tall enough to hide her.

Jax landed a little way ahead of her. He wriggled back. 'I thought you were tricking,' he panted, 'cos I was winning.'

'Shhh!' said Cora, wondering if the Ruffin would hear them. Ruffins had funny rounded ears that didn't work as well as her own pointed ones, but even so! She forced herself to breathe slowly and more quietly. 'What's he doing here?' she whispered. 'Scarlet said the barn wasn't used any more.'

Jax raised his head a pip. 'No idea. Unless he's up early to watch the sun rise. Trix and Nis saw some Ruffins up on Downy Hill when they were working there a while ago.'

'They should stay in their houses until daylight!' grumbled Cora. Luckily, the Ruffin was going in a different direction to the Keepers, heading away from the Whispering Woods. Cora stood up. Now the danger had passed, she noticed something else. 'Corn on the cob with husks! Scarlet will love these.' Cora snatched up the left-behind pieces of corn complete with long whiskery outer leaves. She handed some to Jax and stowed the rest in her woodland bag.

'Let's have a look in the barn,' said Jax. 'See if we can work out what the Ruffin was doing there.'

'Jax, no!'

Jax ignored Cora and sprinted over.
The barn door was open a little and he slid
inside. Cora's chest tightened until she could
hardly breathe. Ruffins spelled trouble but
Jax was her best friend. She couldn't let him
investigate alone. Forcing her legs to work,
she followed him inside. The barn was dusty
and dark. It smelt of rotten wood, old straw
and something else . . .

Cora's stomach turned over. Ruffins!
A whole family, camping in the barn.

'Jax!' Cora's trembling legs could hardly
hold her up. The Ruffins were in the middle
of the barn, not far from a huge ladder
that reached up to a platform in the roof.
Three Ruffins – one woman and two
children – plus the one that had gone for a
night-time wander. They were cocooned in
long bags with hoods and, to Cora's relief,

they were all sound asleep. An empty bag,
unzipped and rumpled, completed the line.
Cora grabbed Jax by the arm and pointed
back to the door. Jax nodded and they
silently tiptoed outside.

'Run!' said Cora.

'Running,' said Jax.

In the distance a low horn sounded.

'Tyr!' Cora gasped. The ancient Viking
horn was a warning to the Keepers to hurry
home before the Bramble Door was shut
and locked.

Cora and Jax ran faster, keeping up the
pace until they reached a group of other
Keepers with bulging woodland bags, also
returning to the Whispering Woods. They
tagged behind them.

'Fully trained Keepers,' Jax said proudly.

'That we are!' Cora agreed. 'No more
school for us.'

They queued in a long line of Keepers waiting to file through the Bramble Door. Once inside the Hidden Middle they went straight to the store where they waited again, this time for Scarlet and Haru to empty their woodland bags.

Scarlet beamed when she saw the corn on the cob. Pulling away the outer husks, she pushed them back over the counter. 'Take these along to the school, please. Signor Dragonfly will want them to make corn Keeper dolls for the Harvest Celebration.'

Every year, in autumn, the Keepers celebrated the countryside and all it provided with a huge feast held by the brook in the very centre of the Hidden Middle. The food was carried to the feast in grass baskets made especially for the occasion. After the parade and before

the feast, Grandmother Sky, the Queen
of the Hidden Middle, awarded a prize for
the best basket.

'I'll take the husks to Signor Dragonfly.
You go and bag us a table at the Crow's
Nest,' Cora said to Jax as they left the
stores.

'No need. We were back before you.
We went to the Crow's Nest and got some
snacks to share,' said Trix, appearing at
Cora's side. Nis was with her and they were
both carrying trays laden with food and
drink. 'Blackcurrant smoothies, acorn crisps
and cupcakes topped with whipped nettle
cream. Fresh today,' added Nis.

'Yum,' said Cora.

'Let's have a picnic by the brook. Then
afterwards we can get started on our basket,'
said Trix. 'I've been thinking about how
to make it extra special.'

The school was just along from the brook. As Cora and her friends walked together, Trix, who loved designing and making things, talked about her ideas. Everyone's favourite was her suggestion to make a basket on wheels so that they could push it along.

'That's brilliant, Trix!' said Cora.

'Definitely a winner,' said Nis.

Trix rolled her eyes. 'It doesn't have to win. It just has to work.'

'Winning is good too!' said Jax, nudging her.

'What are we going to fill it with?' Cora asked Nis.

Nis, who loved cooking, lit up. By the time they reached the brook, he was still describing all the different and lovely foods they might take to the feast. Reluctantly, Cora peeled off towards the school, running over the wooden bridge that spanned the brook. Her stomach did a fluttery dance as she approached the five-storey building with twisty staircases and many balconies that was built among the branches of an ancient sycamore.

School seemed a little smaller now she was a fully trained Keeper. Cora climbed up the outer staircase and entered the main door at first-branch level. Lessons had started and Cora found Signor Dragonfly and his class of seniors in the nursery, helping the little ones to make corn Keeper dollies for the Harvest Celebration.

Her old teacher was thrilled with the corn husks. 'Thank you, Cora. It's good to see you working so hard these days. Perhaps you learned more than I thought when you were here.'

Cora fought back a giggle as she
remembered the last Harvest Celebration
when she and Jax had still been at school.
Had Signor Dragonfly also remembered
the incident with the exploding marrow?
She hadn't meant to drop it and Jax hadn't
meant to kick it either. The whole thing
was a genuine accident.

She was about to leave when she
suddenly recognised a figure sitting at a
desk, patiently helping a little one to
shape a bundle of damp
cornhusks with a length
of grass string.

Cora's mouth
fell open.
'Penelope!' she
exclaimed.
'What are you
doing here?'

Chapter Two

Cora's least favourite person, Penelope Lightpaw, had been in the same class as Cora at school. To Cora's dismay, Penelope had passed her training and become a fully trained Keeper ahead of her. But only because Penelope's best friend Winnie had helped her. Penelope was bossy and very lazy and she always let Winnie do most of the work when they went rewilding in the Big Outside.

Cora couldn't resist. 'Have you been sent back to school?' she asked.

'I'm helping out,' snapped Penelope.
'Because I want to.' Her face softened as the
little one she was working with pushed a
half-finished corn Keeper doll with string
trailing from it towards her.

'Rose, that's brilliant!' Penelope tapped
her thumbs together in praise. 'It's going to
look good on your basket. Shall I tie the
string for you?'

Nodding furiously, Rose gave Penelope
a toothless smile.

Penelope beamed back at her. 'Put your
finger there and press down hard.'

Cora stared, barely recognising this
kind, patient Penelope. She wondered about
it as she returned to her friends. At school,
Cora remembered, Penelope had been
excellent at art and craft. She was only
grumpy and unmotivated when made to do
anything sporty or work in the Big Outside.

Cora couldn't imagine anyone not liking the Big Outside, but the more she thought about it, the more she realised everyone was different, including her friends.

Trix loved engineering, Jax liked to race and Nis was a brilliant cook. Cora was mad about animals and working in the Big Outside. A picture of the Ruffins sleeping in the barn popped into Cora's mind and she shivered. *But* did *she love working in the Big Outside?* Suddenly she wasn't so sure.

'Cattywumps!' Where had that thought come from? Tidying up the woodland pond had been great fun. She wasn't going to let the Ruffins stop her from caring for the countryside. If she and Jax didn't finish clearing the fallen leaves away they would rot, releasing chemicals and reducing the amount of oxygen in the water, and

that could harm the wildlife growing and
living there.

'I love working in the Big Outside!'
Cora said firmly.

'Talking to yourself?' Jax called out as
Cora crossed back over the bridge.

Cora's face flushed. 'Food!' she said
quickly. 'Feed me now, before I starve.'

Jax handed her a blackberry smoothie
and a nettle cream cupcake.

'Yum!'

As she ate, Cora watched Trix scribbling
pictures of baskets and making notes in her
leaf-page notebook. A long while later, Trix
looked up with a satisfied smile.

'Well? Can you build us a basket with
wheels?' Nis asked.

'*We*,' stressed Trix, absentmindedly
scratching her head with the end of a
strawberry-infused red pencil. 'Yes, *we* can.'

Trix showed everyone a picture of a rectangular woven grass basket. It had four wheels and a plaited grass handle that arched over the top. She then set Jax and Nis to work plaiting grass together for the basket and handle. Cora was asked to plait a long length of grass into a rope for pulling the basket along. Meanwhile, Trix went to the stores and came back with some wood

that had once been a tree, before it blew over. Using a saw from her toolbox, she cut out four wheels. Then she used a plane to smooth down the edges.

Nearby, Winnie was working alone on a basket. After a while she came over.

'I love your wheels,' she said, her voice full of envy.

'Why don't you put wheels on your basket too?' said Trix generously.

'Can I? You don't mind me copying?' When Trix nodded, Winnie unexpectedly hugged her. 'Thanks, Trix!'

'That was kind,' said Jax, when Winnie went back to her basket.

Trix shrugged. 'Even with wheels our baskets will be different. Poor old Winnie. No doubt she'll do all the work and then Penelope will come along and take half the credit.'

Cora started to say something about seeing Penelope helping the little ones to make corn Keeper dolls when Jax pounced on her and tickled her ear with a feather.

'Feather fight!'

'JAX!' Cora rolled away, giggling. Spying another feather nearby, she snatched it up. By the time she and Jax declared a truce, Cora had forgotten all about Penelope. She'd also forgotten her Ruffin worries.

They only came rushing back again that night, as she wriggled down under her leaf duvet. Cora lay in the dark, her head filled with pictures of the Ruffins camping out in the barn. She knew she wouldn't sleep until she'd had a hug so she got up and hovered outside her mum's bedroom door. Mum had worked all day in the Crow's Nest. Her snores were louder than a Ruffin's stamping feet. Not wanting to wake her, Cora went looking for Nutmeg instead.

Unusually, there was no sign of her friendly mouse, who lived in the roots of their tree-house home. Cora drifted back to bed, where she lay awake listening to the creak of the branches and the wind rustling through the amber leaves. Finally she fell asleep, but she woke early with a plan. Stumbling out of bed, Cora washed, dressed and made some bark-bread toast for breakfast. She wrote her mum a note, then, still munching on her toast, she hurried down the stairs that spiralled around the outside of the tree trunk. She ran to Jax's house without stopping.

'You're early.' Jax had only just got up and was eating leaf flakes from a bowl when Cora rapped on his door.

'Am I?'

'You know you are. Is this a plan to avoid the Ruffins?'

'No.' Cora gave Jax a look. 'Maybe. How did you guess?'

'They scare me too.'

Jax's honesty made Cora feel a little better. He finished eating then grabbed his woodland bag.

'Hi, lo, off we go.' He took the stairs, riding down the handrail for speed. Cora, her green hair flying behind her, slid after him.

They were so early they beat Scarlet to the Bramble Door. They waited, Cora hopping from one foot to the other, for her to arrive to unlock it. Scarlet was infuriatingly slow, fumbling with the key-shaped twig then returning it to her pocket before she delivered the Want and the Warning.

'Kernels, nuts, berries and anything tasty for the Harvest Celebration feast. *Stay out of sight and don't get caught by the Ruffins.*'

'No way, not today . . . or any day,' Cora promised as she and Jax finally stepped out into the Whispering Woods.

They went straight to the site of the pond, creeping past the barn in total silence. As they approached the pond, a shadow passed over them.

'An owl,' Cora breathed.

The owl had huge white wings dusted with gold. Silent as fallen snow, it flew over Cora and Jax.

'It's a barn owl.' Jax watched the owl with longing. When it had gone, he sighed. 'Imagine flying.'

'Jax!' Cora preferred not to!

Cora and Jax got stuck into work. More leaves had fallen in the night and were floating on the surface of the pond. Jax hooked them out with his net then flicked the wet leaves at Cora. One landed on her head, covering her eyes like a too-big hat. Water trickled down her nose.

For a moment, Cora forgot about finishing the task quickly. She threw the soggy leaves back at Jax then, spying a nearby blackberry bush full of plump purple berries, she scampered over. Cora picked some berries and carefully stowed them in her bag before going back to Jax.

'Purple fingers,' she said, wiggling her blackberry-juice-stained fingers at him.

'Purple nose!' she added, diving at Jax and making a purple splodge on his nose.

'Yum,' said Jax, his eyes crossing as he tried and failed to lick away the blackberry juice with his tongue.

'Now you're making it worse!' Cora cracked up laughing when Jax gave in and rubbed at the stain with his long fingers.

'Purple whiskers!' Jax struck, painting Cora's cheeks with streaks of blackberry juice. They messed around for a while longer then cleaned their hands and faces with water from the pond.

'We should finish our work,' said Cora. 'There are a few more leaves to clear and we should trim the brambles while we're here before they spread any further.'

They gathered the remaining leaves from around the pond and then attacked the brambles, cutting them back and stowing the prickly tendrils in their stretchy woodland bags. The bags were made from spiders' thread and soaked with magic so they could stretch to fit anything inside – even a barn full of Ruffins if Cora ever wanted to move one.

Jax rubbed his tummy. 'Yum! There are enough brambles here for bramble crunch.'

'And there's the blackberries for jam, crumble and smoothies,' said Cora, patting her own tummy. 'I'll finish the bramble bush; you go and start on the seedlings.'

Winged seeds from nearby sycamore trees had taken root right on the edge of the pond. If the trees were left to grow, their leaves would fall into the pond. The trees might also leak other compounds in the water that could harm the wildlife.

Cora lifted her spade and brought it down hard on a trailing bramble.

Something shot from under the bush and
ran past her legs.

'Mouse!' said Jax.

The tiny field mouse dived into a clump
of bushes. Cora was about to attack the
bramble again when she spotted the edge
of a plastic wrapper. She sighed. She hated
the feel of plastic, but when Keepers found
Ruffin rubbish, they were supposed to
clear it up. That meant leaving it by a
Ruffin bin, and if there weren't any nearby
then the rubbish had to be taken
back to Scarlet.

Cora reached for
the nasty plastic
and her chest
tightened.
For a pip
she couldn't
breathe.

'Jax!'

'What's up?'

'There's a second long-tailed field mouse. It's stuck inside the Ruffin wrapper.'

From the opening at the top of the red packet, a long scaly tail dangled. Cora carefully lifted up the edge of the plastic. She saw two tiny white feet attached to a furry brown body and the tips of two round ears. Her heart banged in her ears.

'*Nutmeg?*'

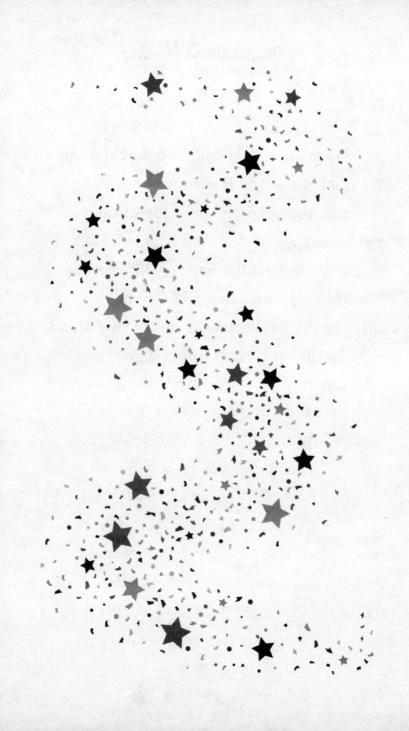

Chapter Three

Jax dropped his spade. He rushed over
to help Cora open the wrapper wider.
Inside the tomb of plastic, the mouse lay
very still. Cora touched it, her fingers
lightly brushing its soft brown fur. Unlike
its friend, this mouse didn't stir.

'Not Nutmeg.' For many terrible
seconds, Cora had thought the mouse was
her very own Nutmeg. Then she'd come
to her senses. Nutmeg never left the
Hidden Middle. Her fur was a lighter
brown, her tail was shorter and anyway,

this mouse was a boy. Cora swallowed.
'I think he's dead.'

Jax crouched down beside her. 'He must have suffocated. Let's get him out of the plastic.'

Together they eased the wrapper away. Cora's heart ached for the little creature. She stroked his cheek. The mouse's nose twitched. Cora blinked. Had she imagined that? She touched the mouse again. Another twitch and the slight quiver of a whisker.

'He's alive!' said Jax.

'Barely,' said Cora. She held her hands over the mouse. 'He needs a sprinkle of woodland magic to help him.' Cora pictured her magic falling on the mouse, getting his lungs working fully. She wiggled her fingers and watched as a sparkly mist fell on the mouse. The magical mist crackled then dissolved but the mouse didn't stir.

Cora tried again and this time Jax helped, combining his magic with hers. Had they done enough? Suddenly the mouse took a tiny gasp of air. Then another, his nose wrinkling as he struggled to breathe.

Cora's hopes soared as she and Jax peppered the mouse with more woodland magic until, with a splutter, both hers and Jax's magic dried up. Frantically Cora wiggled her fingers again but nothing happened.

'Cora, stop! You know you'll have to wait for your magic to recover,' said Jax.

'There isn't time,' wailed Cora. 'The mouse needs help now. I'm going back to ask Scarlet for a healing remedy.'

'What about our task? We won't finish it if you leave,' said Jax.

Not finishing the task would mean another trip past the Ruffin barn tomorrow, but if there was a chance to save the mouse, Cora had to take it – didn't she?

A sycamore seed spun down from a tree, its tiny wings whirring, until it landed by Cora's feet. Absentmindedly she picked it up and put it in her woodland bag. She had to try to help the mouse, however dangerous or scary.

'The Ruffins might be gone by tomorrow. I'm going home to get some medicine.'

'I'll come with you,' said Jax.

'Someone has to stay with the mouse.' Cora desperately wanted Jax to go with her, but they couldn't leave the mouse alone. If Jax stayed, his magic might recover enough to help the mouse if he took a turn for the worse.

'Let me go then. I'm faster than you and I love running.'

Cora stared at Jax, knowing that he was right but unable to get past the guilty rush of relief she felt at the thought of not having to pass the Ruffins in the barn alone.

'Not arguing,' said Jax. 'You're much better at looking after animals than me. See you in a pip.'

In a rush of air he was gone, his hair streaming behind him in a blue banner.

'Stay safe,' whispered Cora.

When Jax was out of sight, Cora took some sycamore leaves from her bag then scraped some moss away from a fallen branch. She tucked the leaves and moss around the mouse, making him a soft nest. The creature barely stirred. Cora was eaten up with worry. What if the mouse didn't survive until Jax returned? What if the Ruffins stopped Jax from returning?

Cora watched her shadow appear, growing longer in the grey pre-dawn light. At last she caught the unmistakable patter of feet.

'Jax.'

'The very me! Scarlet gave me a special tonic. Self-heal and spearmint, infused with woodland magic. She also let me borrow a sunflower seed dropper to help us give it to the mouse.'

Cora waited impatiently as Jax pulled the medicine out of his bag, removed the stopper and sucked a drip of the sparkly pale green liquid up into the sunflower seed pipette. He handed it to Cora.

Cora shook her head. Much as she wanted to be the one to heal the mouse, it wasn't fair. Jax had taken the risk to get the medicine.

'Go on! You're much better at this sort of thing than me,' said Jax.

They both knew she wasn't. Cora might love wild animals more than Jax did, but he was just as capable as her.

'Thanks,' she said gratefully, taking the dropper from him. Carefully she prised the mouse's mouth open and squeezed a drop of liquid onto his tiny tongue.

The liquid poured out. Cora used a finger to help it back into the mouse's mouth. Then suddenly he swallowed. Cora squeezed another drop in, grinning at Jax as the mouse swallowed again. Instead of short raspy gasps, the mouse began to breathe properly.

'He's going to be fine.' A beaming Jax tapped his thumbs at Cora. 'Well done.'

'Well done, *you*,' she said, tapping her thumbs back at him.

They sat with the mouse, waiting until his eyes were bright and his little pink nose twitched inquisitively. He eyed Cora and then Jax. He thrust his nose into each of their hands as if to thank them. Then, with a cheeky flick of his tail, he scampered away.

Cora couldn't stop smiling.

Jax looked up at the lightening sky. 'Time to go.'

Cora's happiness was suddenly tempered with worry. They'd have to come back again tomorrow. But thank the forest they'd saved the mouse, she quickly reminded herself.

They hurried home to the Hidden Middle. To Cora's relief, there were no early rising Ruffins out and about and they passed the barn safely. At the stores, they queued with Trix and Nis to have their woodland bags emptied by Scarlet and Haru.

'Hmmmm!' said Scarlet as she went
through Cora and then Jax's bags.
'A sycamore seed, leaves, blackberries,
brambles *and* you helped a mouse. Good
work, you two.'

'We didn't finish our task,' said Cora,
feeling the need to confess.

Scarlet's lips curved as she fought back
a smile. 'You'd have needed wings to do
everything. No matter. You can finish it
off tomorrow.'

Snoring snails! thought Cora as Scarlet
shooed them away. A tiny mouse-shaped
part of her had hoped that Scarlet would
ask someone else to finish the task. But that
wasn't Scarlet's way. Cora resigned herself to
making yet another trip past the Ruffins!

Chapter Four

Cora and Jax met up with Trix and Nis and they went to the Crow's Nest. Sitting on the top floor, tucking into daisy cream puffs and fizzberry smoothies, Cora soon forgot about tomorrow's task. The Harvest Celebration was happening the following afternoon and Trix wanted to test their basket.

'We know the wheels work when the basket is empty, but what about when we put food in it? It might tip over.'

'Dad lent me a marrow and some apples to try it out,' said Nis.

Exchanging a look, Cora and Jax smothered their giggles. Clearly Nis's dad hadn't heard about their exploding harvest-marrow incident.

Once they'd finished their snacks, they collected their basket from Trix's house. Nis carried the marrow, Cora and Jax the apples and Trix pulled the basket to a long, flat stretch of ground behind the stores.

'Looks like Penelope and Winnie had the same idea,' said Cora as they arrived.

'What the forest!' Trix spluttered. 'Their basket's going to tip up when they put things in it. The wheels are all wrong.'

The wheels looked fine to Cora. Instead, her eyes were drawn to a pair of corn Keeper dolls tied to the front of the basket. One doll had pink hair and was wearing a floaty dress. The other, with yellow hair, wore dungarees. There was no doubt about it – the dolls, skilfully

crafted from corn husks, were made in the exact image of Penelope and Winnie.

Winnie was piling shiny brown conkers into the basket while Penelope watched her. The basket had two handles, one on each side. They were decorated with flowers and plaited grass but there was no rope to pull the basket along. When the conkers were loaded up, Winnie went to the back of the basket and started to push.

'Typical Penelope, letting Winnie do all the work,' observed Jax.

'But . . .' said Cora, her eyes on the intricate corn dolls which clearly had been made by Penelope and must have taken her ages.

'The wheels are wobbling,' said Nis.

'Fizzing frogs! What did I say?' Trix groaned. With a loud clatter, one of the front wheels fell off and rolled away. The basket slumped, its front corner hitting the ground with a bang. It spun in circles, spitting out conkers, forcing everyone to duck and dodge or be hit by a flying nut.

'That would make a great weapon for fighting against Ruffins,' said Jax, when the empty basket stopped spinning.

Winnie ran after the wheel and picked up the conkers. Next she set about repairing the damage. Meanwhile, Penelope

stamped around, scuffing up the leaves
with her feet.

'Let's try our basket,' said Trix.

The four friends lined up along the
length of the plaited grass rope.

'Hi, lo, GO!' Trix called out.

They started off at a walk that turned
into a jog, then a run as Jax, who was at the
front, forgot it wasn't a race.

'Watch the marrow!' shouted Nis, letting go of the rope to stop the marrow from bouncing out.

'We're going to win!' whooped Jax when they reached the end of the flat ground.

'The prize is for the best basket, not the fastest one,' Trix reminded him. She patted her purple hair, fastened in a bun, and pulled out a screwdriver. 'Ours needs a few adjustments before we enter it into the parade.'

'Can we help?' asked Nis.

'Yes. Look after the marrow and apples,' said Trix.

Cora knew Trix and her few adjustments. They were bound to take ages.

Nis put the marrow and apples under a tree. Then, moving a safe distance away, he started a leaf fight with Jax. Cora joined in, throwing crisp gold leaves at her friends until they all looked like tiny trees. They sat on the grass, picking leaves from their clothes and hair.

'What's Penelope doing?' asked Nis.

Penelope was on her hands and knees searching in a patch of long grass.

'Not helping Winnie, as usual,' said Jax. 'I don't know why Winnie puts up with her.'

'We're not helping Trix,' said Cora.

Jax looked at Cora in surprise. 'Trix doesn't want our help.'

'Winnie might not want Penelope's help either.'

'Let's ask her.' Jax and Nis jumped up and went over to Winnie.

Cora heard all three of them chuckle. They talked for a little longer, then Jax and Nis got either side of the wheel and held it in position while Winnie fixed it back on the basket.

Cora stood to offer her help just as her foot uncovered something in the leaves. She picked it up. It was the corn Keeper doll with the yellow hair. Cora went over to Penelope, who was still searching in the grass, and held out the doll.

'Are you looking for this?'

Penelope glared up at Cora. 'Yes!'

'It's Winnie, isn't it?' Cora asked.

'What if it is?' Penelope snatched the doll from Cora's hands.

A picture of Penelope, patiently helping the little one in the nursery, flashed into Cora's head. She hid a grin. Penelope could act all prickly and bossy but Cora had seen another side to her. 'It's clever. I love it,' she said.

Penelope's eyes narrowed, then her expression softened. 'Thanks,' she said gruffly.

Once Trix had finished tinkering with their basket, she, Cora, Jax and Nis spent the rest of the day weaving bits of grass and collecting golden leaves, nuts and seeds to decorate it.

Inspired by Penelope, Cora wanted to make some corn dolls. She even went to the stores to beg some corn husks from Scarlet. But in the end, she didn't have the patience for it. She only managed to make one doll, Trix, and when the head fell off for the third time, she gave up and took the half-finished attempt back to the store so that Scarlet could reuse the corn husk.

Penelope arrived just as Cora was leaving and Cora heard her ask for more corn husks and some feathers for Signor Dragonfly.

That night, Cora was too tired to think about Ruffins. After feeding Nutmeg some seeds from the pot of mouse treats she kept by the side of her bed, she fell asleep immediately. Getting up the following morning was much harder. Cora hid under her leaf duvet wishing she could stay there and not have to finish her task.

But Cora was a fully trained Keeper and determined to be a good one. Trying not to think about Ruffins, she got ready and went to call on Jax. Scarlet was impressed to see them up so early for a second day running.

With the Want and the Warning ringing in their ears, Cora and Jax set off, reaching the pond without seeing a single Ruffin! They got straight to work. It took longer than Cora had hoped but eventually the area surrounding the pond was clear of fallen leaves, newly rooted seedling trees and brambles.

Cora was delighted. 'Now the plants

and animals will have clean water and a
safe space to grow and live in!' She crossed
her hands and offered them to Jax. He
crossed his hands too and they spun each
other round in circles to celebrate a job
well done.

Afterwards, they cleaned their tools and
put them in their woodland bags along with
the leaves, brambles and tiny trees they'd
pulled up.

'Home,' said Cora, doing a happy dance.

Jax slid her a look. 'It's still early. See that
log over there?' He pointed to a slender tree
trunk lying on the ground. 'We could use
it to make a seesaw.'

'Jax!' Cora's stomach knotted. 'What
about the Ruffins?'

Jax glanced over at the barn, just visible
between the saplings, and sighed. 'I guess.
Another time then?'

'Definitely!' agreed Cora.
'Just because we're fully
trained Keepers, it doesn't
mean we can't have fun.'

They crossed
back over the field,
stopping to pick
up a few more
wizened corn-
on-the-cobs, some
dried leaves and a stone with a hole
through the middle.

'Good haul.' Cora patted her woodland
bag.

'Very good haul.' Jax dived and picked
up a husk of corn and popped it in his bag.
'Race you back?'

Cora opened her mouth to agree when
the silence was broken by a long piercing
screech.

Chapter Five

'What was that?' Cora swung round to stare at Jax.

Jax's eyes were huge and his voice wobbly. 'The owl?'

Cora shook her head. 'Barn owls are quiet birds and when they do make a noise it's spookier, more like a hissy snore. That was a scream. Jax, you don't think . . .'

She had to take a deep breath before she could carry on. 'What if it was a Keeper? What if one of us has been captured by the Ruffins?'

'Too loud,' Jax argued. 'A Keeper couldn't scream that loud.'

'Loud enough to be a Ruffin though, celebrating because they'd captured a Keeper,' Cora suggested. The thought made her heart hammer like a woodpecker. *Run*, thought not-nice Cora. *Run to the Hidden Middle as fast as you can.* But nice Cora had other plans, and before she could stop herself, nice Cora was saying, 'I'm going to find out. Someone might need our help.'

Jax tugged at a strand of long blue hair. 'It didn't sound like a Ruffin. Ruffins are loud but a lot more shouty. Let's just go home.'

Another screech filled the air, even more distressed than the first.

'It's coming from Downy Woods.' Cora lifted her chin. 'We can't walk away and do nothing. There'll be lots of places for us to hide among the trees.'

Jax sighed. 'Hurry up then.'

Changing direction, they headed for Downy Woods. It wasn't hard to follow the screeches because they were coming more frequently now. Cora broke into a run. If the noise was a captured Keeper, they might be able to help, like Jax, Trix and Nis had the time they'd rescued her from the Ruffin child. But only if the Ruffin wasn't keeping watch. The thought made Cora's head feel hedgehog-prickly and she stopped looking where she was running. Her foot clipped something hard. The object spun away from her. Cora lost her balance and fell forward. Putting out her hands to save herself, she landed flat on her face in a pile of leaves.

'Poo!' said Jax. Rocking with laughter, he pulled up beside her.

Fear had been squeezing Cora's insides like bindweed. Now laughter burst from her

mouth and she clapped it shut, covering it
with her hands as she giggled. 'Poo yourself!'

'No, poo! I thought you tripped over a
lump of poo,' Jax explained. He kicked up
the leaves with his foot. 'But luckily for you,
it's only an owl pellet.'

Cora eyed the grey pellet warily. What if
she'd been mistaken and the screeches *were*
being made by an owl? Owls were hunters

and could easily mistake a running Keeper for a scurrying mouse. What if they were running towards a different sort of danger?

'We've come this far,' said Jax, guessing her thoughts. 'Whoever is making that noise is in trouble. If we can help them then we should.'

He offered Cora a hand and pulled her to her feet. Jax claimed the pellet and stuffed it in his woodland bag. Nothing was wasted, and owl pellets often contained lumps of fur and tiny but useful animal bones. They set off again, slowing their pace to a fast walk as they neared the source of the screeches.

'We're not far from the river,' said Cora. Her ears were picking up rushing water. Then, as the trees thinned, she caught a flash of blue.

Jax stopped suddenly. 'Listen.'

In silence, they stood side by side. The

screeches sounded just as panicked but somehow quieter, the cries of a creature fighting a losing battle.

'Over there.' Cora darted forward, creeping towards a tree with a slender light grey trunk. 'It's an owl, on the ground. Look, Jax, it's tangled in something.'

The barn owl was flapping around by the roots of the tree. A length of blue Ruffin fishing line snaked around her white underbody, looping back over her golden wings and pinning them to her sides. There was more blue cord binding her long legs together. The owl strained against the plastic twine as she desperately tried to escape. Cora winced when the bird gave another hissy screech.

'She'll die if we don't help her. We need a stone to cut her free.' Cora searched the ground.

Jax looked around and found two sharp flints. 'Here,' he said, handing one to Cora.

Silently they approached the owl from behind. Not silently enough. Her head swung round. Large panicked eyes in a heart-shaped face stared them down. Cora and Jax dived into a clump of tall weeds, then froze. Barn owls had excellent eyesight. They could sense the tiniest of movements. Their hearing was exceptional too. Cora began to question her decision. What were they doing, thinking they could help? Owls were dangerous and might see a Keeper as a tasty snack.

As if to prove her point, the owl hopped towards their hiding place. The fishing line stopped her, tightening around her legs and making her screech again.

Cora shoved her doubts away. They couldn't do nothing.

Before she lost her confidence, Cora made a dash for the bird, sprinting up behind her.

Jax followed and overtook Cora. Scrambling onto the owl's back, he attacked the fishing line behind the owl's wing with his flint.

The owl's head turned again. Jax sawed faster. Cora climbed up to help him. It wasn't easy. The owl's soft feathers were slippery and difficult to hold on to.

'Careful,' Jax warned. 'Once we've freed her wings she'll fly away. Be ready to jump.'

'I'd better work on her legs then,' said Cora, trying not to look at the owl's sharp talons. The owl wouldn't survive for long in the Big Outside with her legs still bound together.

They worked in silence. The fishing line bit into Cora's hands, creating red welts. Cora felt even sorrier for the bird. She must be in agony too. A trickle of moisture ran down Cora's face. She stopped for a second to wipe it away. Gritting her teeth, she set to work again, hacking through the nylon fishing line.

At last the line started to fray. Encouraged, Cora pressed harder. Fibres pinged under her flint until only a few remained. This was a dangerous moment.

'Be ready for her to start hopping around,' Cora warned Jax as she reached in to cut the final strands.

Chapter Six

The line twanged as it broke. Cora leapt back, ready to run. The owl, still trailing a long piece of fishing line from her other leg, started to hop forward. She was clearly trying to fly but she couldn't open her wings.

'Wings or other leg?' Cora called up to Jax.

'Help me with the wings,' said Jax.

Cora wasn't sure it was the right decision, but either way they were putting themselves in a lot of danger now the owl had more movement. Soft feathers brushed her cheeks and nose as she set about hacking through another stretch of the fishing line. Her flint wasn't as sharp now and Cora had to put more effort into her work as she sawed at the nylon.

'I'm not getting anywhere,' said Jax. 'The line is so tangled it's hard to know where to cut it.'

'I'm not getting very far either,' Cora admitted. 'How about we try some combined woodland magic?'

'Good idea!' said Jax. 'I'll come to you.' He climbed over the owl's back to reach Cora. They perched behind a wing and held out their hands, their long fingers pointing at the owl's feathers. In her mind, Cora pictured the fishing line unravelling.

'Ready?' Jax whispered. 'Hi, lo, *go!*'

Cora and Jax wiggled their fingers, creating a sparkly magical mist that hissed and popped as it melted into the taut fishing line. For a moment nothing happened, then the line began to fray.

'It's working!' breathed Cora, watching as the line dissolved.

'Jump!' yelled Jax.

The last thread of plastic fishing line pinged back, leaving two broken ends which cracked like a whip as they flew out. In the pip of time, Cora ducked, grabbing at feathers to stop herself from sliding down the owl's back.

'Cattywumps! We did it.' But the owl was on the move again. Frantically, she flapped her free wing in an effort to fly away.

'Now for the other wing.' Jax scrambled back over the owl.

As she climbed after him, Cora knew that this wasn't going to end well. The fishing line was still tied around the bird's tail and leg. How could they untangle it all before the owl flew away?

'Cora?'

'Here.' Cora went to help Jax. Her fingers tingled as they combined their magic and a fine sparkling mist fell on the line. This time, as it broke, Cora was ready and ducked out of the way.

'We did it!' she said, tapping her thumbs at Jax.

'Next we need to free her leg and tail,' said Jax.

As Cora had suspected, now the owl had control of both of her wings, she had other ideas. Flapping them vigorously, she created an enormous downdraught of air that knocked Cora over. She lurched sideways into Jax, sending him flying like an acorn skittle. Cora couldn't save herself and slid down the owl's back. She landed on the ground.

Jax was sliding too, headfirst along the owl's tail. 'Help!'

Cora gasped. Jax's foot had snagged in some fishing line. He held out his hands to Cora but as she reached up to pull him down, the owl began to rise.

'Jax!' Cora had to stop the owl from flying away with her best friend. She ran and lunged, grabbing hold of the fishing line trailing from the owl's leg. She stood firm with her legs apart, bracing herself as she leaned back. Was she strong enough to stop an owl? The fishing line tightened and Cora was thrown from her feet. Still hanging on to the line, Cora scrambled up, only to be knocked down again by the owl's tail. She bumped across the ground as the owl flew up into the air. The owl rose quickly. Suddenly Cora's stomach arrived in her mouth as the ground beneath her rushed away.

'I'm flying!' Too frightened to think straight, Cora pedalled the air with her legs, as if that would save her! Arms burning, she dangled from the end of the fishing line. Cora looked down, wondering if she could jump, but already the ground was too far away – and what about Jax? She couldn't leave him. Cold air blasted her face and her eyes smarted. Blinking until she could see again, Cora looked up, searching for Jax

↘OPERATION **OWL**↙

among the owl's feathers. There he was! The right way up and hanging on for his very life. With a spark of panic, Cora realised her arms were tiring. She couldn't hold on for much longer.

'Cora, climb up here.'

The line swung wildly as Cora squinted at Jax, who was reaching out a hand to her.

'Climb up the line,' he yelled again.

Could she? Cora forced herself to breathe slowly. If Jax thought she could do this, then she could! Uncurling her fingers, she slowly began to pull herself up. There. That wasn't so bad. A little further and she'd be able to touch the owl's feathers.

'Watch out!' Jax cried.

Too late, Cora saw the tree. While the owl skimmed gracefully over its crown, Cora wasn't so lucky. She hit a branch and was jerked backwards. Snatchy twigs snagged her clothes. Cora hung on tightly to the line, hoping the bird would be strong enough to pull her free, but Cora's fingers were losing their grip. The fishing line tore through her hands, stinging like the bite of a red ant.

'Jax!' With a yelp, she plummeted.

Colours flashed before Cora's eyes: the blue of sky; the red, orange and gold of leaves; the blue of sky . . .

The ground came closer. Cora's vision blurred, but instead of splattering, she felt a jerk and then she was spinning face down in a circle. Slowly and carefully, Cora looked up. Her shirt had caught on a twig.

'Cora!' Jax's cries faded as, on ghostly white wings, the owl carried him away. Cora grabbed hold of another twig, using it to twist herself round to watch the owl. On it flew, over Downy Woods and then a field. *Their field!* The one they'd crossed earlier. Cora could just make out the roof of the barn in the distance. Numb with shock, Cora imagined the worst. She would never see Jax again. She couldn't see him now. Jax was far too small. Cora watched as the owl changed course and flew to the barn. It reached the apex of the roof and disappeared inside.

A loud ripping noise brought Cora back to her own predicament. *RIP!* A tear appeared in her shirt. The tear lengthened and suddenly the material gave way.

Cora gasped. 'Cattywumps!'

Chapter Seven

Twigs brushed Cora's hair as she crashed through the tree. Some of them snapped and she fell in a flurry of leaves, pinging from branch to branch. Every bump, every jerk, Cora felt them all until she was out of branches. Suddenly she was in freefall. Her long hair, trailing behind her like a parachute, did nothing to slow her down.

Cora landed with a crash in a huge pile of crisp autumn leaves. Her breath whooshed out in a noisy rush. She closed

her eyes, breathing in the mushroomy smell
of the autumn woodland as the world spun
around her.

Every single bone in Cora's body ached,
but she wasn't splatted – or a snack for an
owl. It was Jax, her oldest and best friend,
who was in mortal danger.

Cora stood on wobbly legs, then she ran
through the woods and out into the field.
It seemed twice as wide now. She stumbled
on, leaping over the dried-up furrows until
finally she arrived at the barn.

For a pip she slumped against it, her
chest heaving. A loud snore shattered her
rest. *The Ruffins!* How could she have
forgotten about them? Cora had hoped
to use the ladder inside the barn to reach
Jax. But maybe she could climb up the
outside of the building and enter through
the same hole as the owl?

Cora leaned back and sized up the barn. It was timber built and with proper climbing stuff, like a rope and hooks, she could probably get to the hole. But she didn't have the right equipment.

With a feeling of dread, Cora realised the only way to reach Jax was by the ladder. The barn door was shut. Cora nudged at it with her toe and felt the wood give. No wonder the farmer didn't use it any more, the wood was rotten.

Cora kicked it again and this time her foot went straight through. She held her breath, listening for signs that the Ruffins had heard the splinter of wood. No one stirred. It was now or never. She stepped through the hole.

'Cora!'

Cora spun around. For a wild pip of a second, she thought it was Jax calling her, but then Trix and Nis came racing towards her across the field.

'We were on our way home when we saw you. Where are you going so fast?' asked Trix, hopping through the hole after her.

'Where's Jax?' Nis added as he joined them.

Putting a finger to her lips, Cora pointed at the Ruffins, four of them today, cocooned in hooded sleeping bags like giant caterpillars. Motioning for Trix and Nis to follow, she tiptoed across the barn and took cover behind the wheel of a rusty Ruffin tractor. Quickly and quietly, Cora explained what had happened. Trix and Nis gasped and when Cora had finished speaking, Trix immediately said, 'We'll help!'

Cora hesitated. She badly wanted and needed her friends right now, but at the same time she didn't want to put them in any danger.

'Don't argue,' said Nis.

'I didn't!'

Nis grinned. 'You were going to! It was stamped all over your face. We're helping and that's that. We've finished our task and found six of Scarlet's Wants. It's not long until sunrise. Admit it, you need us.'

Cora grinned. Her friends were the best. 'I don't have a plan other than climbing up the ladder to reach Jax.'

Trix had been scoping out the barn. 'The big ladder over there, behind the Ruffin camp?'

They tiptoed over. It was made from wood and went up to a platform beneath the roof, scattered with broken straw bales. Cora shoved her hands in her pockets, her hopes plummeting.

'Look at the gap between each rung. It's far too big for us to climb.'

'We'll find a way.' Trix drew her notebook from her pocket and a mint-infused pencil from her hair. She sat cross-legged on the ground, her pencil flying across the page.

On silent feet, Cora searched the barn for anything that might help them. She

found a length
of twine, the
sort the
Ruffins used
to tie up
their hay
bales. Nis
joined in and
found a pile
of wood, in
lengths that were

much too small for the Ruffins to bother
with. Lastly, Cora found a metal button with
a grooved edge.

'Let's take this stuff to Trix, she might be
able to use it,' said Cora.

Trix had covered her page with pictures
and notes. One of her ideas involved a
pulley to help them climb the ladder. Cora
got excited. She and her friends had used a

pulley once, to rescue a deer stuck in a
ditch on a new housing estate.

'We can make a pulley with the button
and twine.'

Trix shook her head. 'A pulley needs
someone at the bottom to do the pulling.
The twine isn't long enough either.'

'What then?' Cora asked.

Trix picked through the wooden offcuts.
Cora counted to one hundred in her head.
The barn was slowly growing lighter. It
wasn't fair to let Trix and Nis stay. She
would tell them to go before Scarlet locked
the Bramble Door and they were shut out
of the Hidden Middle.

But as she went to speak, Trix whispered,
'I've got it!'

Chapter Eight

Trix held up two equal-sized lengths of wood. 'We'll *make* a ladder.'

Cora stared at Trix in confusion. 'We've already got a ladder. It's too big.'

'Exactly. So, we make a smaller one with hooks at the top. We hang it from the first rung of the big ladder and climb up it. At the top, we unhook it and hang it from the second rung. Then we climb up that and so on.'

Nis grinned. 'Genius! A ladder to climb a ladder.'

'Genius!' echoed Cora.

'It shouldn't take long to build.' Trix was already rummaging in her woodland bag. 'This is why I never go anywhere without a few essentials. Scarlet's extra-strong glue,' she muttered, pulling out a hollowed-out acorn full of glue and a saw.

Trix began by cutting two lengths of twine, one much longer than the other.

'These are my rulers,' she told a mystified Cora and Nis. 'The shorter one is to measure the rungs and the longer one is to measure the side rails.'

Using the longer length first, Trix cut two pieces of wood to the same size for rails. Then she carefully measured the wood for the rungs with the shorter length of twine. Cora and Nis took it in turns to cut each rung to the right size.

Soon they were all covered in tickly sawdust. Cora had to bury her nose in her

arm to stop herself from sneezing out loud.
Nervously she eyed the Ruffins. None of
them stirred and the biggest one was snoring
loudly. Trix assembled the pieces of wood on
the floor in the shape of a ladder, then glued
it all together.

'We need hooks,' she said, glancing up at
Cora and Nis. 'Don't worry if you can't find
anything hooky enough – I can make some
from the leftover wood.'

Quicker if we can find something, Cora
thought. She glanced over at the Ruffins
and their makeshift camp. They weren't
very tidy and they had a ton of stuff. Cora's
fingers itched to go and have a rummage.
The Ruffins would surely have something
they could use. But tempting as it was, it was
wrong. Keepers were only allowed to take
Ruffin items that had been left behind or
were littering the Big Outside. Reluctantly

turning her back on the mountain of Ruffin stuff, Cora began to search the barn.

'I've got something,' whispered Nis. He was standing by a plastic Ruffin bucket with a hole in the bottom. Cora, who hated the feel of plastic, had passed it by without a glance, but Nis had noticed that the bucket had a metal handle.

'The handle has two hooks to attach it to the bucket,' Nis explained.

It took some nifty saw work and the combined woodland magic of Nis and Trix to cut the hooks from the handle.

'Definitely worth it,' Nis said, panting.

'Definitely,' Trix agreed. 'There,' she said,

fixing them to the top of the ladder with the twine that she'd used to measure the wood and a splodge of Scarlet's extra-strong glue. 'It just needs a pip to dry.'

Cora could barely stand still. Now there was nothing to do, all her thoughts turned to Jax. He was in so much danger. What if the owl saw him and decided he'd make a tasty snack?

Trix examined the ladder. 'It's ready. It looks safe but I'll go first.'

'No!' said Cora, a pip too loud. She couldn't let Trix and Nis stay any longer. Daylight was on the way and besides, it was far too dangerous. 'The ladder's brilliant, Trix. Thanks for building it, but you and Nis should go home now.'

'Squeaking squirrels, you're not rescuing Jax alone!' said Trix.

'Safer together,' Nis agreed.

'Anyway, the ladder was my idea. I should go first to test it.' Trix muscled her way past Cora. 'You two keep a look out for both the owl and the Ruffins.'

A warm glow spread through Cora. 'Fine,' she said, 'but I'm going first, Trix.'

They locked eyes.

Nis sighed. 'Move out of the way, Trix, and let Cora through. We're wasting time.'

Cora shot Nis a grateful look as she started up the ladder.

Nis crossed his finger over his thumb. 'Good luck!'

'Good luck to us all,' whispered Cora. Her legs felt wobbly, especially as she climbed higher. It was the scariest thing she'd ever done, even more scary than when the Ruffin child had trapped her. That time she hadn't had a choice. She'd just had to get on with things.

⌄OPERATION **OWL**⌄

Now she was putting her friends in the face of two unpredictable dangers!

Cora climbed faster until she reached the first rung of the Ruffin ladder. Nis and Trix were right behind her, panting like foxes. They all took a second to get their breath then hauled  their ladder up so they could attach it to the next rung. On they climbed.

Halfway up, Cora stopped. *What was that?* Hissy grunting sounds were coming from above her. *Ruffins*, Cora decided. Were there more Ruffins camping up in the roof? She cupped her hand to her ear.

'Listen!' she mouthed to Trix and Nis.

It wasn't easy to hear above the hammer of her heart. If it was Ruffins then at least they were asleep! The weird, hissing snores grew louder the higher Cora climbed. Soon there was only one rung left to go. Cora went up it and arrived on the platform in the roof. The broken straw bales littering the platform smelt musty. Cora's nose tickled and she rubbed it vigorously, determined not to sneeze. Quietly, she stepped forward. A flash of blue, half buried in a straw bale, caught her eye. *Jax?*

It *was* Jax! Cora was about to rush over when Trix grabbed her arm.

'Wait!' she whispered. 'We're being watched.'

Chapter Nine

'Owlets!' breathed Cora.

'Giants!' said Trix.

'Nearly ready to fledge,' Nis added.

The three baby owls were almost as big as their mother but the golden feathers along their heads and backs were brushed with a darker downy fluff. They were sitting a short distance from mum on a pile of hardened owl pellets. They were communicating with funny hissing and snoring sounds. Cora gawped at their long legs and scaly toes with sharp curved

talons. Signor Dragonfly had taught them about owlets. Cora wished she'd paid more attention in class. She might have been better prepared to help Jax if she had.

Trix put a finger to her lips then tapped on either side of her face. Cora stared. Then suddenly some of Senior Dragonfly's lesson came back to her. Barn owls didn't have outer ears, like Cora's pointy ones. Instead their heart-shaped faces helped to direct sound towards ear openings just behind the owl's eyes – exactly where Trix was tapping on her own face. Owls had exceptionally good hearing, if Cora remembered rightly, especially for higher-pitched sounds, like the squeak of a mouse.

The biggest owlet suddenly flapped its wings, sending tiny clouds of white fluff into the air. Curiously it leaned forward, pushing its face at Cora, Trix and Nis.

Cora swallowed a shriek as she and her friends scuttled behind a bale of straw. They stood in silence, hardly daring to breathe. Cora imagined the owlets listening out for them in the same way they were listening out for the owlets.

Cora was the first to move, slowly inching around the straw bale. Trix and Nis went with her. At the bale's raggedy edge,

Cora stopped. From here she had a clear view of the owlets and their mother.

The mother owl was still tangled in fishing line. The nylon was stretched taut around one leg and her tail. They couldn't leave her like that. It would be too easy for her to get snagged in something.

'I'm going to have to try to remove it,' whispered Cora.

'Not without me!' Jax silently appeared at her side.

'Jax!' Cora hugged him. 'You're safe. I was so scared when you flew away.'

'Me too, at first, but then . . . flying by owl . . . it was brilliant!' Breathlessly Jax started to recount his adventure.

Trix stopped him. 'No time,' she whispered. 'Let's get the owl untangled and get out of here before Tyr sounds or the Ruffins in the barn wake up.'

'Now Jax is here –' Cora started, but Trix and Nis both shook their heads.

'Safer together,' said Nis firmly.

'And fairer. Four of them and four of us,' said Trix. 'Nis and I could distract the owlets while you and Jax untangle the mother.'

It was a good plan, the best they had, but time wasn't on their side. Cora knew this was their last chance to help the owl. She felt in her pocket for the piece of flint Jax had given her earlier. Curling her fingers around it made her feel braver. She'd got this.

Cora and Jax tiptoed behind the straw bales, creeping up on the owl from behind. The open space between them and the owl was huge. Could they really cross it without being seen by the sharp-eyed owlets?

'Ready?' asked Jax.

Cora nodded. Breaking cover first, she ran to the owl. As she ran, something whizzed over her head. A straw bomb! The owlets' heads whipped round as the bomb hit the floor and exploded. It was a marvellous distraction that wouldn't hurt them. The straw bombs came thick and fast, leaving Cora and Jax with a free run to the mother owl.

'Watch out for her tail!' Jax hopped clear as the owl stirred and almost knocked him over.

Cora's heart fell when she saw the amount of knotted fishing line still tangled in the owl's feathers.

'See this bit here?' Jax pointed. 'If we can undo that knot, the rest should come free.'

'How though?' Cora picked at it with her nails. It had pulled tight and was as tough as old bark. It would take ages to cut through it with their flints.

'Woodland magic?' Jax suggested.

'We can try.' Cora cleared her mind of everything except the owl. She hoped her magic would be strong enough now she hadn't used it for a while. 'Ready?' They had to be quick. Trix and Nis could only keep the owlets distracted for so long.

'Ready,' Jax whispered.

Cora held her hands over the knot, her outstretched hands almost touching Jax's. To her relief, a magical mist fell from her fingers, combining with Jax's magic to create a swirling, sparkling cloud that covered the knot in the fishing line. Cora willed the knot to unravel, then held her breath as the misty magic crackled and

hissed. *Snap!* The line broke. Cora and Jax
tugged it, carefully pulling it free from the
owl's feathers. The owl whipped her head
round. Her warning hiss sent shivers
skittering through Cora. A piece of twine
was stuck. Cora and Jax tugged harder.
The owl struck, stabbing her open beak at
Cora and Jax.

'Pull!' shrieked Cora.

'Pulling!' yelled Jax.

Cora put her weight into it. The line
finally pinged, its free end whipping back.
Ducking out of the way, Cora and Jax
darted to safety across the dusty floor, each
dragging an end of the twine behind them.
Their straw bale seemed a forest away. The
owl came at them. She opened her beak.
They weren't going to make it! A straw
bomb whooshed over Cora's head. *Bam!*
It landed between her and the owl then

exploded. The air was cloudy with pieces of straw and dust motes.

'Almost there!' Cora panted as she and Jax sprinted to safety. They collapsed in a heap behind the straw bale, holding on to each other until their breath caught up with them.

'Good work!' mouthed Trix, lobbing her last missile over the bale of straw.

Neatly, Jax coiled up the two lengths of fishing line and stowed them away in his woodland bag, keeping an eye on the owl as she hopped over to her owlets.

'Job done,' said Cora. 'Time to go home.'

Chapter Ten

Cora, Jax, Trix and Nis ran back to the tiny ladder attached to the top rung of the larger Ruffin one. Their descent was much faster than their climb up. Working as a team, each time they reached the next rung of the Ruffin ladder they silently unhooked their tinier one and attached it to the lower rung before climbing down it again.

'Ruffins,' Cora warned Jax as they neared the ground. Jax wiggled his fingers back at her to show he'd remembered.

There was one rung left to climb down. For the last time, they unhooked and reattached the ladder. Cora was the last to go, but as she stepped out, she heard a rustle. Cora stared. To her horror, the noise was coming from the Ruffin camp. Someone was awake! A Ruffin sat up, blinking. She was a small child, with a soft round face and big eyes, but she was still enormous compared to the Keepers.

Transfixed, Cora couldn't move. The Ruffin child had sleep-rumpled hair that stuck out in all directions. *Like mine*, thought Cora, running a hand through her tangled green locks. The girl peered around. Her gaze fell on the ladder, moved on, then snapped back. She leaned forward, rubbed her eyes, then stared again. Her huge mouth opened.

Cora was mesmerised. If the Ruffin screamed, they were done for. She waited,

staring back at the girl, bracing herself for her to shout for the adults. But instead, the girl smiled. Then very slowly she lifted a huge hand and waved.

In her surprise, Cora almost fell from the ladder. Quite without meaning to, she waved back. Even from a distance, Cora saw the Ruffin child's face light up.

 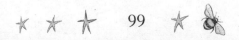

'Cora!' Jax's voice floated up to her. Jax, Trix and Nis were waiting on the ground, unaware that the Ruffin child had woken. 'Get a wiggle on!'

'Wiggling,' Cora whispered back. She gave the girl one final wave before starting down the ladder. Reaching the bottom, she glanced back at the Ruffin camp, still not convinced the girl wouldn't come after her. But the Ruffin girl was tucked up in her sleeping bag, her eyes closed. Cora couldn't stop staring. What had just happened?

In the distance, a horn sounded.

'The Horn of Tyr!' said Nis.

Cora snapped out of her daze. 'Time to go home,' she said.

On the way back, Jax didn't stop talking, telling everyone over and over again about his adventure. He kept stopping to act out how he'd used the rope like a swing to right himself before pulling himself up the owl's back so that he could sit between her wings. His face glowed with excitement as he described his dizzying flight and how wonderful the view of the Big Outside was from the sky.

'Weren't you scared?' asked Cora, deciding not to mention the Ruffin child so that Jax could have the moment to tell his story.

'A pip,' Jax conceded. 'And my arms ached a lot, but it was worth it.'

Cora didn't even try to understand. Jax was safe and so was the owl. That was all that mattered.

Back in the Hidden Middle, Jax finally stopped bragging about his adventure – there wasn't time with the Harvest Celebration taking place that very afternoon.

Trix had some final adjustments to make to their basket and then it had to be filled with tasty treats for the celebratory harvest feast.

Cora inhaled the delicious aromas. There were freshly baked chestnut-filled wheat puffs from her mum, apple crunch surprise

from Jax's big sister, an edible wheat straw hedgehog from Trix's parents, and a plaited loaf of acorn-and-blackberry bread, golden in colour and still warm, with a pot of acorn butter. The loaf and butter were Nis's creations and they smelt so good it almost made Cora's mouth dribble.

When their basket was ready, Cora, Jax, Nis and Trix lined up with their friends for the start of the grand harvest basket parade.

Looking around, Cora was pleased with
their efforts. Their basket was getting a lot of
attention, not just for its wheels but also for
the plaited loaf and the hedgehog.

The competition was stiff though.
Winnie was next in line and Cora took in
her basket. The wheels were much sturdier
than before and the grass-plaited handles
were decorated with yellow toadflax flowers
and wild white clover. But best of all were
Penelope's corn Keeper dolls. She had
artfully perched them on a mountain of
tiny cakes shaped like mice and oozing with
deep red rosehip buttercream.

'Yum!' said Cora, deciding she had to try
one the moment the feast started.

'Penelope made the cakes,' said Winnie.

'She did?' There was definitely more to
Penelope than Cora had realised. 'Where
is she then?'

'Fixing her hair, I bet!' said Jax, mimicking Penelope by running a hand through his blue locks.

'I'm here.' Penelope appeared at Cora's side. 'I was finishing this. For your basket. But only if you want it,' she added, thrusting a present wrapped in leaves into Cora's hands.

Cora gasped as she opened the gift. Four corn Keeper dolls, with their arms casually slung over each other's shoulders. One doll had messy green hair, another blue, there was a redhead and one whose hair was styled in a purple bun that was skewered with a tiny screwdriver.

'Me, Jax, Nis and Trix.' Cora swallowed hard. 'They're beautiful,' she whispered. 'But why did you make them?'

Penelope shrugged. 'For helping us with our cart. I don't think I would have bothered to help if it had been the other away round,' she added a little too honestly.

Everyone burst out laughing. Penelope looked embarrassed but then she laughed too. 'You're all so outdoorsy and keen. It's exhausting.'

'We are!' Cora chuckled. 'But being different doesn't mean we can't be friends.'

'Really?!' squeaked Winnie.

'I suppose.' Penelope sounded gruff.

'Group hug!' said Cora, throwing her arms out.

They hugged each other tightly until Penelope broke away. 'Watch my hair!' she grumbled.

Cora grinned at Jax as Penelope

pulled a comb from her pocket. What a day of surprises! First the Ruffin child and now Penelope. Was it possible to be friends with a Ruffin? Cora still wasn't sure, but one thing she did know, Penelope was much nicer than she'd realised.

The parade was about to start. Cora sighed happily as she arranged the four corn dollies in their basket. New and old, Cora's friends were very different but they were all brilliant.

The End

✳ The Keeper Way ✳

Be a Barn Owl Detective

While barn owls can be seen during the daytime, they mostly hunt at night over rough grassland. The dark means they have to rely on their hearing to help them to find food, such as field mice and voles. A barn owl swoops down, catches its prey and then swallows it whole, usually head first. Owls can't digest fur or bone so this is then sicked up, in a process called

regurgitation. The regurgitated material comes out as an owl pellet. Owls aren't the only birds to do this – other birds such as crows and buzzards also sick up pellets of undigested food.

A barn owl pellet is black when it's fresh but this changes to grey as it dries out. You can find out what a barn owl had for its dinner by examining one of its pellets. Barn owl pellets are often found near an owl's resting site, which is usually a sheltered place such as in a barn where the bird can hide away to sleep.

A barn owl pellet has no smell. If it does, then you have NOT found a barn owl pellet.

Examining a Barn Owl Pellet

★ Put the pellet on a flat surface and gently pull it apart with your fingers.

★ What did you find? Barn owl pellets usually contain undigested fur and bones. Sometimes they can hold the bones of as many as six small mammals.

* Try and identify any bones by the skull and/or by the jaw bones. You can find pictures of animal bones online or in reference books.

* Remember to wash your hands thoroughly when you have finished.

Hunt Like a Barn Owl

A barn owl's hearing is as sharp as a superhero's. This is to help it to hunt in the dark. A barn owl has two differently shaped ears. They don't have outer flaps like yours do. Owl ears are holes on either side of its heart-shaped face, next to its eyes. One ear is higher than the other. When an owl is flying, its left ear picks up sounds from below, while its right ear hears sounds from above. Combining the different sounds helps the barn owl to work out where its prey is hiding.

Hunt Like a Barn Owl Game

You will need:

★ 4 or more people

★ A scarf or other blindfold

★ A large open space somewhere safe and
  enclosed like a playground or a classroom
  with the desks pushed back.

1. Pick someone to be the owl.
2. Blindfold the owl.
3. The other players are the mice and
   voles.

4. The mice and voles sit in a circle around the owl.

5. Take it in turns for one mouse or vole to run around the owl making squeaking noises.

6. The owl has to try and catch the mouse or vole by listening out for them.

7. When the owl finally catches its dinner, the mouse or vole swaps places with the owl and takes a turn at being the hunter.

Protecting nature is magic for the secret little Keepers

Look out for more adventures from the Nature Keepers.

Julie Sykes

As a child, Julie was always telling tales.
Not the 'she ate all the cake, not me' kind,
but wildly exaggerated tales of everyday
events. Julie still loves telling stories and
is now the bestselling author of more
than 100 books for children of all ages
and is published around the world. She
has recently moved to Cornwall with
her family and a white wolf – cunningly
disguised as a dog. When she's not writing
she likes eating cake, reading and walking,
often at the same time.

Katy Riddell

Katy grew up in Brighton and was obsessed with drawing from a young age, spending many hours writing and illustrating her own stories, which her father (award-winning illustrator Chris Riddell) collected. Katy rediscovered her love for illustrating children's books after graduating with a BA Hons in Illustration and Animation from Manchester Metropolitan University. She loves working with children and lives and works in Brighton.

We hope you loved your Piccadilly Press book!

For all the latest bookish news, freebies and exclusive content, sign up to the Piccadilly Press newsletter – scan the QR code or visit lnk.to/PiccadillyNewsletter

Follow us on social media:

bonnierbooks.co.uk/PiccadillyPress